Jenny's First Sleepover

Written By
Moshe Rhodes

Illustrated By
Kristin Coghlan

ISBN 978-1-7333147-0-1

First Edition published 2019

www.jennysfirstsleepover.com

For Dash and our Dot, who will be vaccinated.

-M

Jenny was turning seven.
She was very excited.
She went to her mom and asked,
"Now that I'm a big girl, can I have a
sleepover?"
"Yes," said her mom. "We'll have a
sleepover for your birthday."
"Yay!" shouted Jenny.
"Yay," said her mom under her breath.

"You can invite 10 friends."
"And grandma?" Jenny asked.
"And grandma," said her mom.

Jenny invited all her best friends to her party.
Polly and Patricia. Taylor and Daphne.
Ruby and Vicki. Mary and Molly.
And the twins Hannah and Hayley.
They all came and brought birthday presents...

But none of them were vaccinated.

Polly brought polio. Patricia brought pertussis.
Taylor brought tetanus. Daphne brought diphtheria.
Ruby brought rubella. Mary brought measles.
Molly brought mumps. Vicki brought varicella.
And the twins Hannah and Hayley brought hepatitis A and hepatitis B.

They had a great time.
Jenny opened her presents.
They sang happy birthday.
They ate ice cream cake.
Jenny's grandma read
them a bedtime story.

"Uh-oh! I forgot my toothbrush,"
Patricia said.
"So did I," said Polly.

"Here, you can use ours," said
the twins Hannah and Hayley.
And then they all went to sleep.

The next morning all of Jenny's
friends went home.
On her way out, Molly tripped on a
rake.

"Ouch!" Molly exclaimed.
"You have a boo-boo on your hand,"
her Dad said.
"It doesn't hurt," Molly said.

Three days later, Molly's mouth was stiff.
"I don't want to eat dinner,"
she said to her Dad.

Soon she started to spasm.

"This could all have been prevented with a vaccine."

Tetanus is an especially painful disease. Muscles spasm uncontrollably. The jaw locks. Eventually breathing is disrupted. In today's United States, tetanus is still fatal in 10% of cases. Thanks to vaccination, the rate of tetanus in the United States has decreased forty-fold, from approximately 4 cases per million people immediately after World War II to <0.1 cases per million people today.

One week later Daphne wasn't feeling well.
She had a fever and a stiff neck.
"My arms hurt, and my legs won't move," she
said to her mom.

Her mom took her to the doctor and the doctor examined her.
"You have polio," the doctor said.
"There is no cure. We can only hope it doesn't get worse."

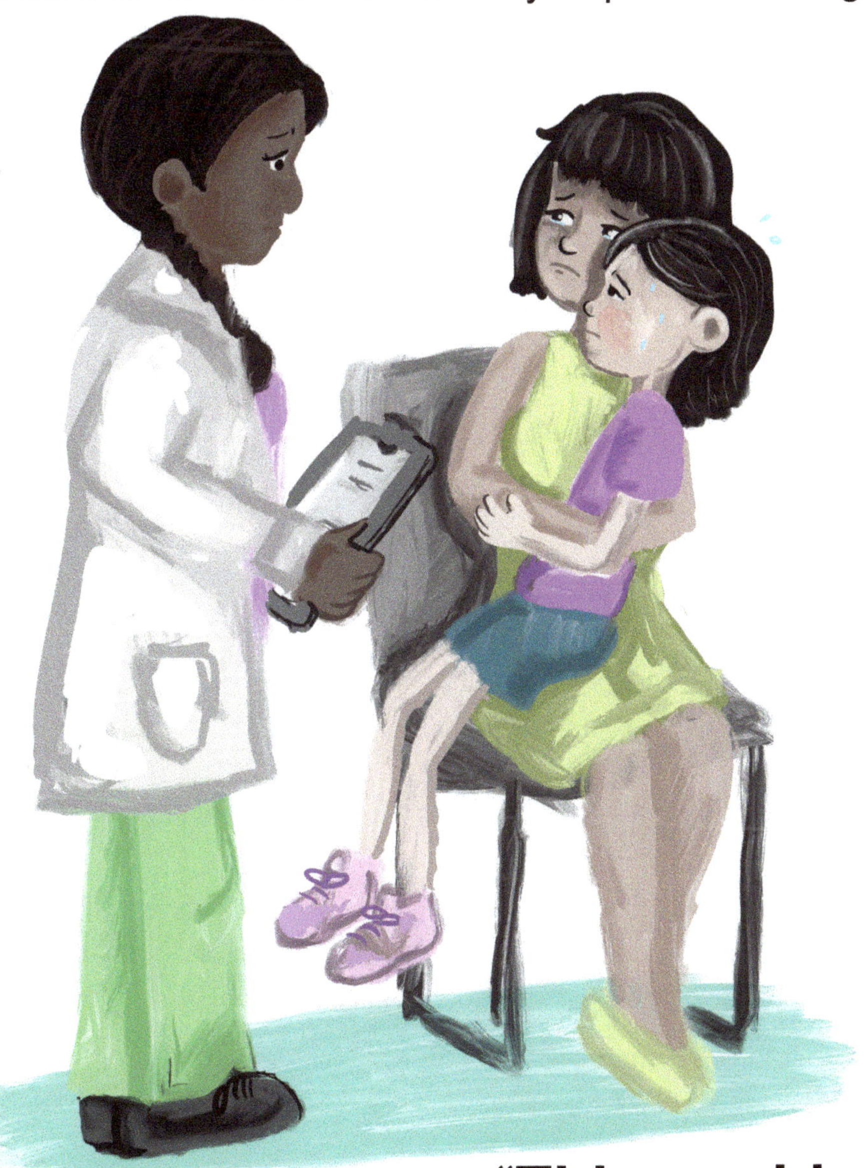

**"This could all have been
prevented with a vaccine."**

A month later she left the hospital,
on crutches for the rest of her life.

Prior to the creation of the polio vaccine by Jonas Salk in 1952, polio epidemics were frequent. In 1952 in the United States alone, more than 50,000 children were infected, leading to more than 3,000 deaths. Of those who survived, thousands more were paralyzed. In 2017, there were 30 cases worldwide.

Mary's throat was sore. She couldn't swallow.
She had so much gray mucus it was hard to breathe.
Her parents rushed her to the emergency room.

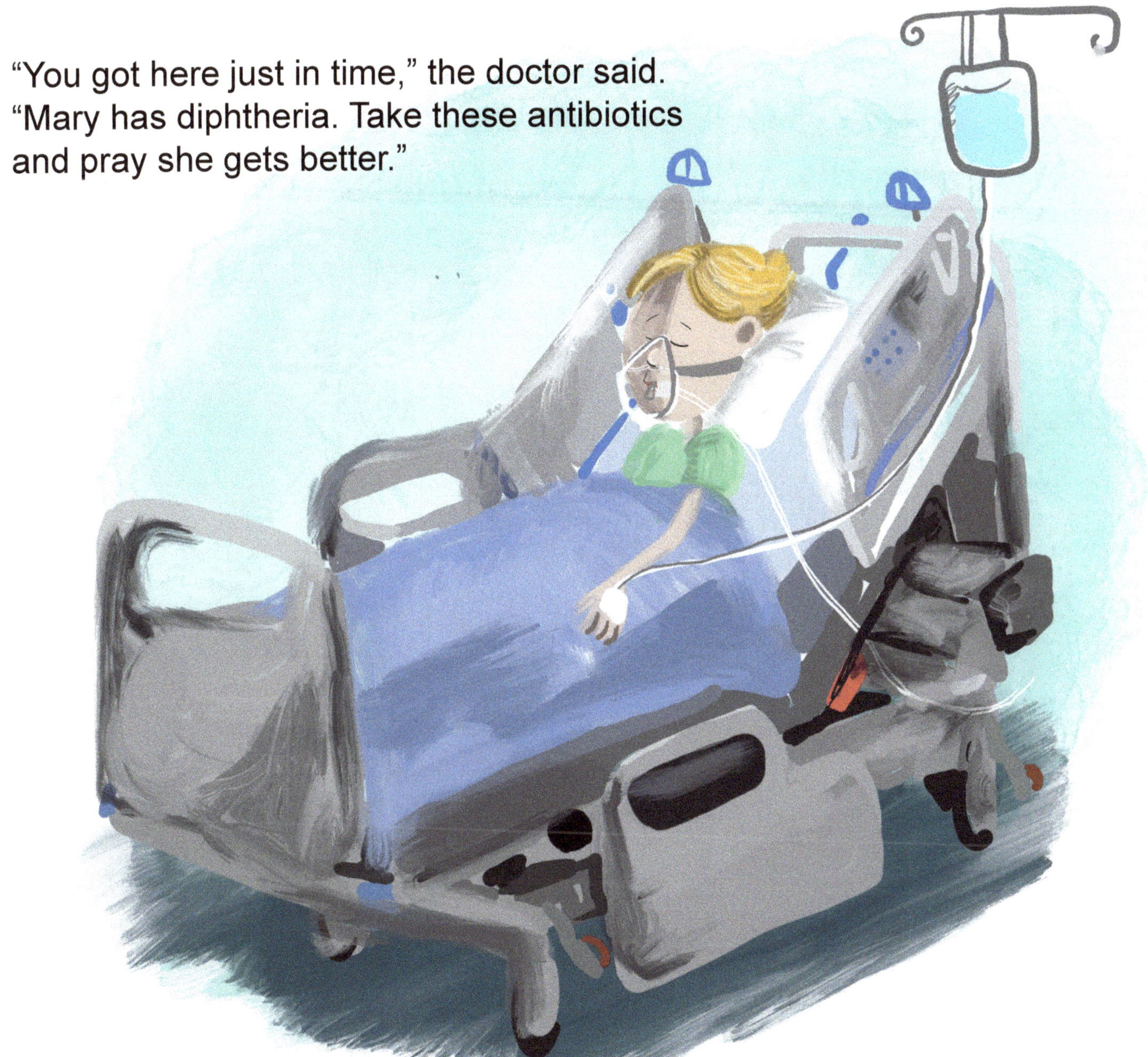

"You got here just in time," the doctor said. "Mary has diphtheria. Take these antibiotics and pray she gets better."

"But remember, this could all have been prevented with a vaccine."

Mary's throat cleared up,
but the toxins had reached her heart.
There was nothing the doctors could do.

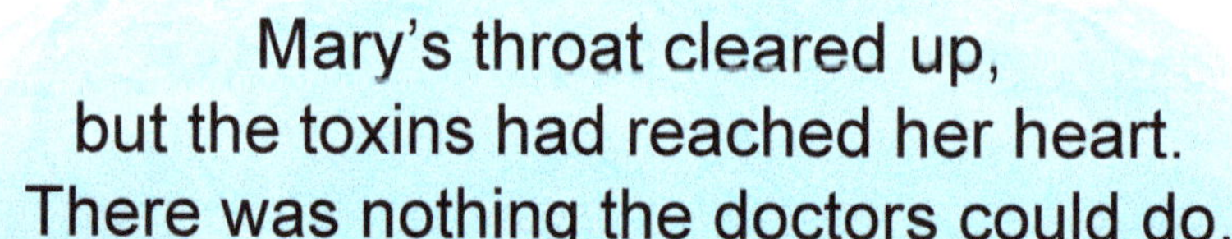

Diphtheria is a child killer. The mortality rate for diphtheria is 3% in healthy adults and up to 20% in young children and the elderly. Due to vaccination, diphtheria has been largely eliminated from the United States. Prior to widespread vaccination there were over a million cases worldwide per year. This has been reduced to approximately 10,000 in 2017.

At Mary's funeral, Taylor started
to cough.

She coughed and coughed and coughed.
She coughed and coughed and coughed.
She coughed for days.
She coughed for weeks.
She coughed so hard she turned blue
and her ribs cracked.

Her parents took her to the doctor
and the doctor examined her.
"Your daughter has pertussis," the doctor said.
"Will she be OK?" Taylor's mom asked.
"It's hard to say," the doctor replied.
"The damage might already have been done."

"This could all have been prevented with a vaccine."

Pertussis is especially dangerous to infants. Even today, it has a mortality rate of 0.5% in infants. Prior to the development of the vaccine in the 1940's there were approximately 200,000 cases in the US annually. A strong vaccination campaign dropped the rate to less than 2000 cases annually in the early 1980s. Over the past three decades, the rate of pertussis has actually increased significantly. This increase is partially due to a shift from the more effective whole cell vaccine to a less effective acellular vaccine with reduced side effects.

Two weeks after Jenny's birthday party,
Vicki had a cold.
Her nose was runny.
Her throat hurt.
She had a mild fever.

But the cold kept getting worse.
Her fever kept going up.
Soon Vicki had a fever of 105ºF, and a red rash had
begun spreading all over her body.

Her mom rushed her to the doctor.
“Your daughter has measles,” the doctor said.
“If we can control her fever, she should be OK,
but measles is highly contagious.”

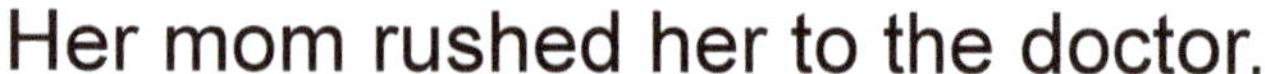

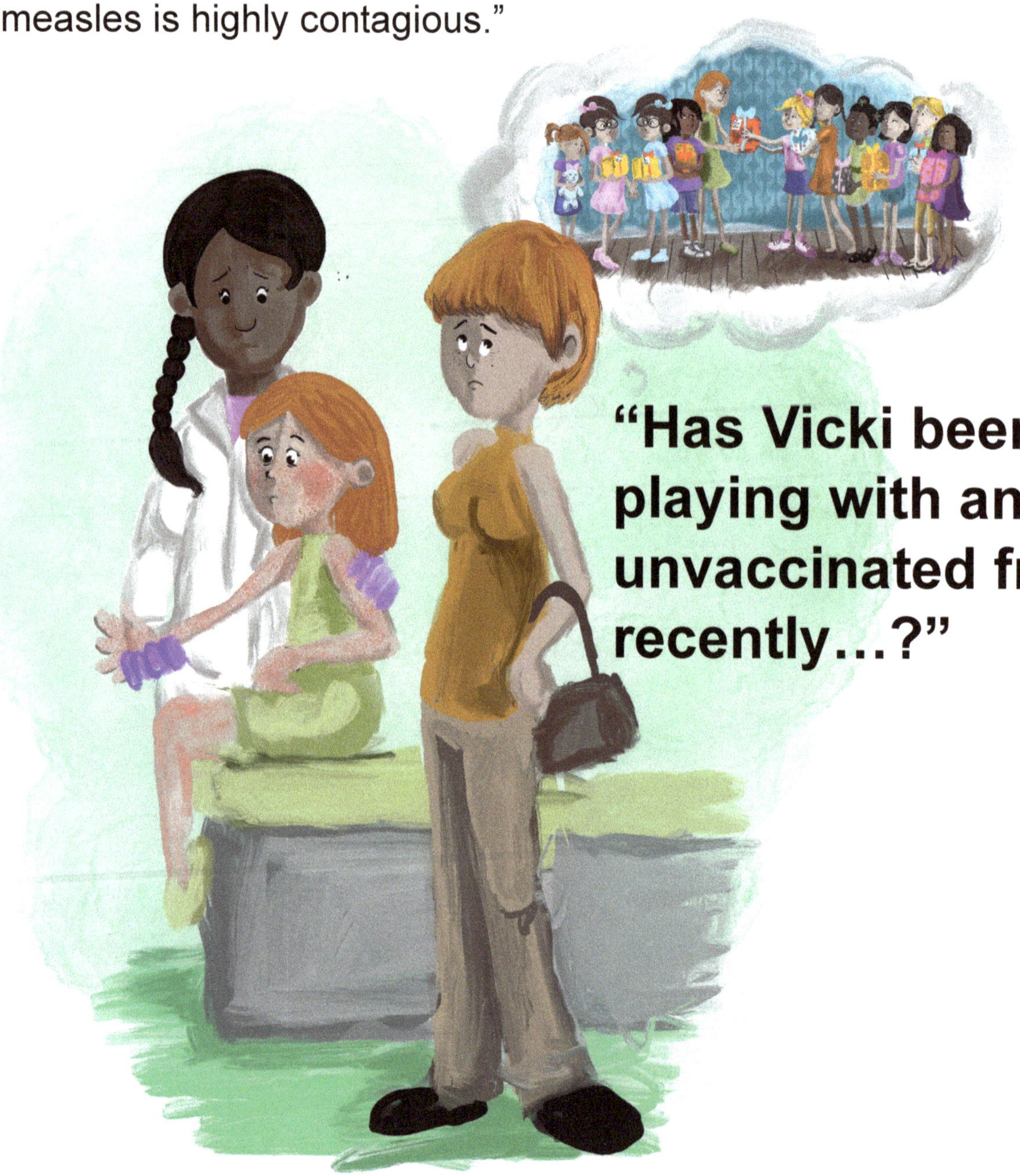

“Has Vicki been playing with any unvaccinated friends recently…?”

90% of susceptible individuals exposed to measles will be infected. In the year 2000, the United States was declared measles free due to an aggressive vaccination campaign. Prior to vaccination, there were over half a million cases in the United States per year. Worldwide there remain approximately half a million cases every year leading to thousands of deaths. In the year 1998, the British doctor Andrew Wakefield published a now discredited research paper claiming a link between autism and the vaccines for measles, mumps, and rubella. This fraudulent claim initiated a backlash against vaccines. Anti-vaccine activism has led to a resurgence of measles outbreaks in the United States, especially in communities with low vaccination rates. Numerous studies have examined Wakefield's claims, and there remains absolutely no credible scientific evidence linking the measles vaccine to autism.

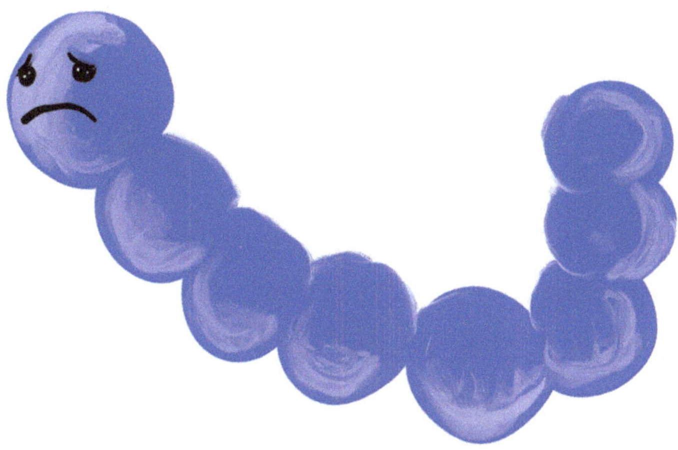

Hannah looked at Hayley.   Hayley looked at Hannah.

"Your face looks funny," Hannah said to Hayley.
"Your face looks funny too," Hayley said to Hannah.
"Let's go show dad," they said together.

They raced to their dad and showed him their swollen necks.
"Does it hurt?" their dad asked.
"Some," Hayley said.
"A little," Hannah said.

Two hours later the twins were in horrible pain. Their dad rushed them to the hospital.

"Your girls have mumps," the doctor said. "It is rarely serious but can be very painful. It should go away in a few days..."

"but remember all the pain could have been prevented by a vaccine."

Compared to many of the other diseases described here, mumps is decidedly less lethal. Its telltale symptom is severely swollen salivary glands. It usually clears up on its own after a few days. Complications, such as swollen testicles potentially leading to male sterility, can occur and are more common in adults than in children. Vaccination has significantly reduced the number of cases in the United States from over 100,000 per year to a couple hundred per year. As with measles, there is absolutely no scientific evidence linking the mumps vaccine to autism.

Polly and Patricia were getting ready for bed.
"Your eyes look yellow," Patricia said to Polly.
"So do yours," Polly said to Patricia.
"What's happening to us?!?" they both shouted.

They ran to their mom who
took them to the doctor.
"Well," the doctor said, "your
eyes are turning yellow
because your livers aren't
working. I think you have
hepatitis."

"Have either of you shared earrings, or
nail clippers, or toothbrushes with anyone
who might have been infected?"

Polly and Patricia thought.

"I used Hannah's toothbrush at Jenny's sleepover," Patricia said.

"And I used Hayley's toothbrush at Jenny's sleepover," Polly said.

"Let's get you tested and see what we find," the doctor said.

Two days later Polly and Patricia
went back to the doctor.
"Patricia you have hepatitis A. Your
liver should heal on its own in a
few months."
"Polly, you have hepatitis B. It is a
much more serious disease."

Six months later Polly and Patricia went back to the doctor...

"You're all better,"
the doctor said to Patricia.
"What about me?" Polly asked.
"I'm sorry Polly," the doctor said.
"Your hepatitis B has become
chronic. You may have permanent
liver damage."

**"This could all have been
prevented with a vaccine."**

Both hepatitis A and hepatitis B are diseases of the liver. Hepatitis A is easier to transmit, but it is much less severe. Hepatitis B can become chronic and lead to permanent liver damage, liver cancer, and liver failure. It is most often transmitted between adults via intravenous drug use or during sexual activity. It can also be transmitted from mother to fetus during pregnancy. Hepatitis B is highly contagious and can survive in microscopic drops of blood, making alternative modes of transfer possible (such as sharing a toothbrush). Prior to widespread vaccination, about 16,000 children under 10 in the United States got hepatitis B each year. Only half of these cases were the result of mother to fetus transmission. Overall, rates of hepatits B have decreased ten-fold (from 200,000 to 20,000 cases in the United States per year) over the past 30 years partially due to vaccination.

Jenny's back was itchy.
She tried and tried to scratch,
but just couldn't reach.

"You have the chicken pox,"
her mom said.
"Make it go away," Jenny cried.
"I can't," her mom said. "Try not to
scratch and it will go away in time."

"I'll call grandma and maybe she can come over and read you a story."

Jenny's mom called grandma, but grandma couldn't come over. She was in too much pain. She needed Jenny's mom to take her to the hospital.

At the hospital the doctor examined her.
"You have shingles," the doctor said. "It
can be very dangerous for people your
age. You must have had chicken pox
when you were younger."

**"These days both
chicken pox and
shingles can be
prevented with a
vaccine."**

Both shingles and chicken pox are caused by the same virus, varicella zoster. Once a person is infected with chicken pox, the virus can remain dormant for decades in the host's nervous system until manifesting as shingles later in life. Both diseases can be extremely uncomfortable but on their own are not usually fatal. Nevertheless, vaccination prevents almost 4 million cases of chicken pox in the United States each year and over 100 deaths. Amongst the elderly, roughly 1 in 3 individuals can expect to get shingles without vaccination. Up to 4% of shingles sufferers will need to be hospitalized.

A month after Jenny's birthday, Jenny's mom wasn't feeling well. She had a mild fever, a sore throat, and a runny nose. In a few days she felt better.

Five months later, Jenny's brother Andy was born.

Baby Andy was born deaf and with heart problems.
The doctor examined him and asked,
"were you sick while you were pregnant?"
"Yes," said Jenny's mom, "I had a mild flu about four months ago."
"You had rubella," the doctor said. "It's not that dangerous but can cause serious birth defects. Andy is now at risk for cognitive disorders including autism."

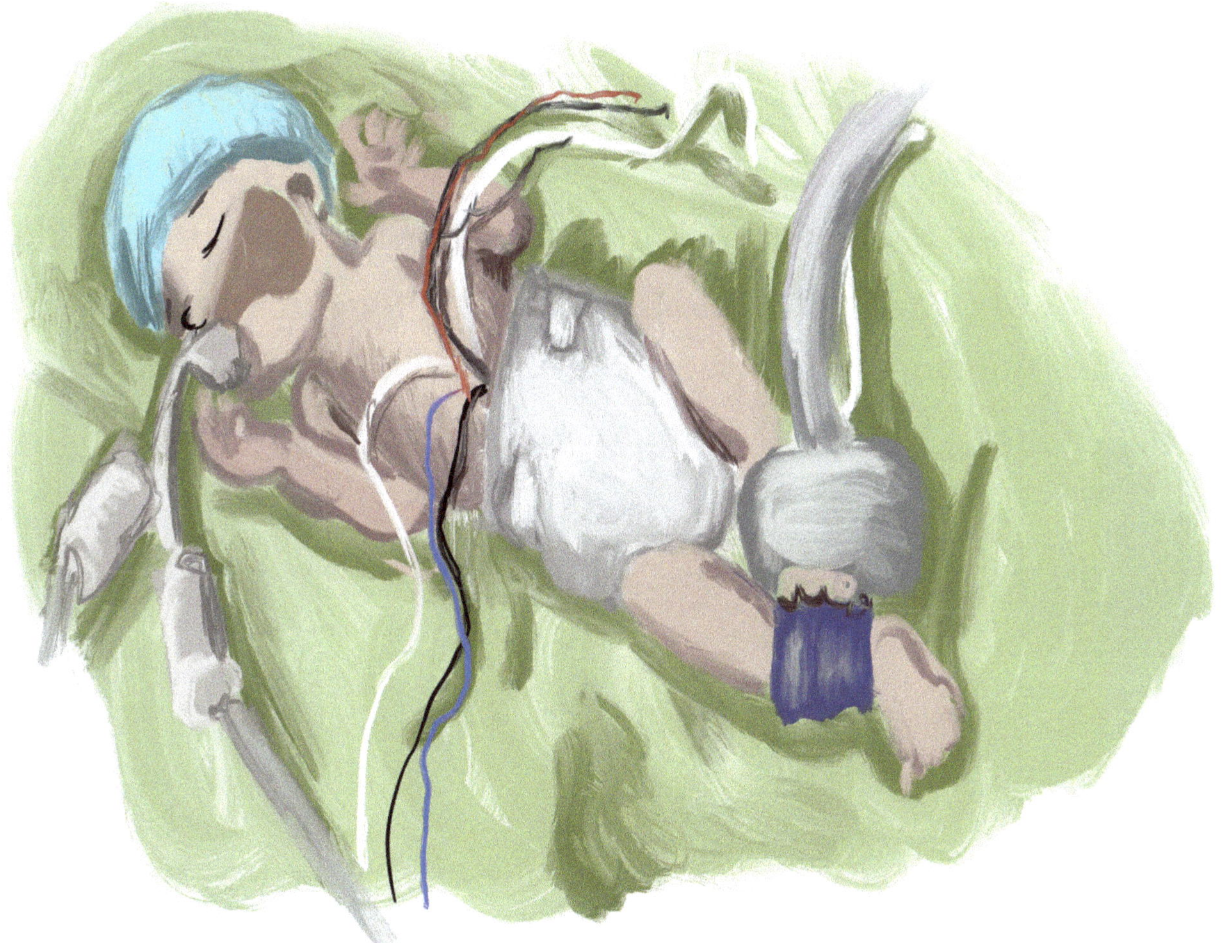

"This could all have been prevented with a vaccine."

Rubella is a relatively mild viral infection. Many individuals infected with rubella don't even realize that they are ill. Possibly the most serious danger of the rubella virus is its impact on pregnant women. Women who contract rubella early in pregnancy are at a high risk of having a child with congenital rubella syndrome. Symptoms include deafness, congenital heart defects, cataracts, and even death. Rates of vaccination for rubella have been decreasing due to the false association of the rubella vaccine with autism. Ironically, one consequence of congenital rubella syndrome can be cognitive impairment including autism. There has been no scientific evidence linking the rubella vaccine to autism.

As with all medical treatments, there is some risk associated with vaccination, but the benefits to society far outweigh the risks. These last examples highlight the fact that oftentimes we are not vaccinated to protect ourselves, but rather to protect the weakest members of our society. A healthy adult has little to fear from chicken pox or rubella. The same cannot be said for innocent pregnant mothers, unborn fetuses, infants, or the immunocompromised, such as the elderly or cancer patients.

Ever since the development of the vaccine for smallpox by Edward Jenner in 1796, vaccination has proven to be one of the crowning achievements of modern medicine. Every year vaccination saves millions upon millions of lives.

Jenny was turning eight. She was very excited.
She went to her mom and asked, "Can I have a
sleepover again for my birthday?"
"Yes," said her mom.
Jenny invited nine friends to her birthday party, and all
of them were vaccinated.

The end.

www.ingramcontent.com/pod-product-compliance
Lightning Source LLC
Chambersburg PA
CBHW041150300726
48981CB00003B/215